DISTRI<

TAKING CONTROL

Katherine Hengel

SADDLEBACK
EDUCATIONAL PUBLISHING

DISTRICT 13

SADDLEBACK
EDUCATIONAL PUBLISHING
www.sdlback.com

ISBN-13: 978-1-61651-276-7
ISBN-10: 1-61651-276-8
eBook: 978-1-60291-946-4

Printed in the U.S.A.

21 20 19 18 17   3 4 5 6 7

1

Marcel stopped in the street. He was the biggest of the three boys. He was also the kindest. Marcel stopped Akil too. "Wait now, Tre," Marcel said. "Best looking girl? In the whole school?"

"You heard me," Tre yelled. He was across the street now.

Akil touched Marcel's arm. "Later,

big man," he said. Then he jogged over to Tre.

"Later, Tre," Akil said. But Tre ignored him.

"Deena is fine," Tre said. "I know it."

"She's okay," Akil said. "See you later."

Akil ran to his building. He climbed the stairs. It was late in the fall. The windows were open. He heard Marcel and Tre arguing. They were out on the street.

Akil didn't think Deena was fine. At all. He disliked her in fact. But Akil didn't argue with Tre. Not anymore. It wasn't worth it. Akil used to be small and shy. Tre took care of him then. But things weren't like that now.

Akil entered his apartment. His mom was on the couch. "Hi, baby," she said.

"Hi, Ma," Akil said. He kissed her cheek. "Long day?"

"The usual," she replied. "You hungry?"

"Nah," Akil said. He walked to his room. He grabbed the notebook under his bed. He returned to the living room. "I ate. Did you? You want anything?"

"I'm fine, sugar," his mom said. "But I'd like to feed you once in a while."

"Ma, I eat."

"Yeah, right," she said. She smiled

at her skinny son. Then she fell
asleep.

Akil sat with his notebook. The
edges were worn. He got every penny
out it.

He stared at a blank page. He
didn't hate all girls. Just Deena.
Deena was a big mouth. But Tre
liked her. So she was always around.
Akil couldn't control that. What
could he control? "Not much," he said
out loud.

2

Akil wanted to sleep. But it was too noisy. He rolled out of bed. Why do people move on Saturdays?

"Look who's awake!" his mom said. She was pouring coffee.

"Who could sleep!" Akil said. He rubbed his eyes.

"Oh, baby! I forgot to tell you! Patrice and her mom are moving back. I just helped them with some

boxes. I gotta run. See you tonight."
She kissed Akil good-bye. She had to
get on her tiptoes!

Akil didn't move a muscle. How
could she forget to tell him? "I need
to change," Akil thought. He ran to
his bedroom. He grabbed a T-shirt off
the floor. It smelled okay. He put it
on with his best jeans. He ran to the
living room window. That window
faced the street.

Akil saw a small moving van.
Patrice's mom was next to it. Where
was Patrice? Akil hadn't seen her
in two years. She moved out with
her mom. Akil never knew why. One
thing he did know. He missed Patrice.

Patrice and Akil grew up
together. They were the same age.

They even went to the same daycare!
Patrice came over after school
too. She ate dinner at Akil's a lot.
Patrice's mom was always "out."

The building's front door swung
open. A tall woman ran down the
stairs. She did so two at time. "That
can't be her," Akil thought. The
woman walked to the van. Patrice's
mom grabbed a tiny TV. She carried
it to the building.

The woman put her hands on
her hips. She looked up and down
the street. Then she ran her hands
over her hair. That's when Akil knew
it was Patrice. She did that all the
time. She always had her hair back.
She always smoothed it out like that.

Akil turned from the window.

"Should I help them?" he thought. His mom would say yes. He turned back to the window. Patrice's mom was back. They each grabbed a box. They locked up the van.

3

Akil called Marcel. He had to tell him about Patrice! "I'll call Tre," Marcel said.

Akil watched from the window. He couldn't wait on the steps. He was afraid he'd see Patrice! He didn't want to step outside! Soon he saw his friends. He ran for the door.

"You fools are lucky," Tre said.

"How's that?" Marcel asked.

Tre pulled out a blunt. It was in his chest pocket. "Damn!" Marcel said. "No way you rolled that."

"You must not want any," Tre said. He put it back.

"Where did you score that?" Marcel asked.

"My cousin Darren," Tre said. "He just got into town. He's got a place in West. Lives with a couple guys."

Akil's heart raced. He had smoked before. But weed made Akil nervous. But he followed his friends. They walked to an alley. Tre lit the blunt. He puffed until it was burning. Then he passed it to Marcel.

The boys each hit the blunt. Then Tre put it out. "Can't let you fools smoke it all," he said. "Akil, let's watch TV at your crib."

Akil agreed. They left the alley. Everything was fine. Until they got to Akil's block.

"There she is," Akil said. He stopped walking. Patrice was at the front door! She had a basketball on her hip.

"Who is that?" Tre said.

"Over here!" Akil said. He ran into the alley. Marcel did too.

"What are you doing?" Tre said. He followed them. "What the hell?"

"I can't see her," Akil said. He was panicked. "It's been two years. No way I'm talking to her. Not this high."

"That's a damn shame," Tre said.

He poked his head out. He looked at Patrice. "That girl is fine."

The boys waited. Patrice walked away. Then they went to Akil's. Akil felt terrible. He pulled out his keys. He opened the door. That's when someone said his name.

There was a man in the kitchen! He held a glass of water. The man smiled.

"Akil, it's me, Uncle Robert. It's been a while, little man. But you ain't so little. Bet you got an inch on me!"

Akil was stunned. "Ah, this is Marcel and Tre," he said.

"Nice meeting you," Marcel said. Tre nodded.

"See ya, Akil," Tre said. Then they ran down the stairs.

4

"It's not forever, baby. And he's family," Akil's mom said. "Will you open this?"

Akil opened the jar of pickles. He handed it back. Uncle Robert had just left.

"You want another mouth to feed? That's up to you," Akil said. He was angry. Why didn't he have any say? He was mad about Tre too. Akil didn't want him talking to Patrice. Or watching her.

Uncle Robert came back in. He was holding a basketball. "You play, Akil?"

"Why, because I'm tall?"

Uncle Robert got quiet. He took a breath. "There's a court down the street," he said. He tossed the ball to Akil. "Want to go?"

Akil looked at his mom. He had no choice. "You coming, Ma?" he asked.

"Nah, I'm gonna rest. You go have fun."

Uncle Robert and Akil went outside. Uncle Robert spoke first. "Bet you got some questions," he said. Akil acted like he didn't. But really he did. "I lost my job, Akil," Uncle Robert said. "Me and thirty other guys. Your ma said I should come here. You know. To look for work."

"You ever been in jail?" Akil asked.

Uncle Robert smiled. "Now we're talking! See that '77 Charger over there? I killed a man for that car. But I got away with it."

Akil smiled at the joke. They walked to the car. "There's rust by that wheel. Other than that, she's a ten." Uncle Robert was proud. He loved his car. Akil bent down. He looked at the rust spot. Then he heard a voice he knew. It came from across the street.

"Are you hiding from me, Akil?"

It was Patrice. Akil stood up. "Hey," he said shyly.

Patrice ran to him. She threw her arms around his neck. Akil dropped the ball. Uncle Robert grabbed it. It would have rolled in the street. "Where you been, Patrice?" Akil asked.

The smile left her face. "At my grandma's," she said. "Who's your friend?"

"This is my uncle Robert."

"Nice to meet you," Uncle Robert said. He held up the basketball. "Join us?"

"Sure," Patrice said. "Akil, do you play at school?"

"Nah, I don't play much. Not like we used to."

They all walked to the court. Uncle Robert passed the ball to Patrice. She stepped toward the baseline. She looked so natural. She shot the ball. Nothing but net. Akil's jaw dropped.

"Can you do that again?" Uncle Robert asked. The answer was yes. And that's what she did. Patrice had a mean jump shot. She drained about a hundred shots. Then the sun went down.

5

They left the court together. Uncle
Robert was excited. He wanted
Patrice to join the team at school!

"You're gonna sign up, right?" he
asked.

"Maybe," she said smiling.

"Not maybe! You got the best
jump shot in this city! And you're
fourteen!"

"Good night, Uncle Robert,"

Patrice said. "Good night, Akil. Don't hide from me, okay?"

"I won't," Akil said. His smile was huge. He knew his uncle saw. But Akil didn't care. He couldn't help it. Uncle Robert smiled too. Then they all went to bed.

Akil woke on Sunday morning. He walked to the living room. A folded blanket was on the couch. "Where's Uncle Robert?" Akil asked.

"He's looking for work, Akil," his mom said. "I told you he would. Remember?"

Akil smiled. Uncle Robert was keeping his word. He kissed his mom. "He played hoops with us last night. With me and Patrice. We all hung out until dark."

"That's great, baby. I'm glad."

Akil was glad too. Uncle Robert was pretty cool. And Patrice! She was perfect! She was the same girl. But grown.

Akil called Marcel. He had to tell him about Patrice. He wouldn't forget this time. They met on the street.

"Man, my night was solid," Akil began.

"Not mine," Marcel said. "I was with Tre. He got tipsy. Real tipsy. He wouldn't shut up. Kept talking about that girl. You know. The one from your building. What he was gonna do and all. He is into her, man."

Akil stared at the sidewalk. His blood was boiling.

"Akil, how does that sit with you? Is she your girl? You better say something. Ya know, if she is," Marcel said.

Akil looked up from the sidewalk. "Where is Tre? Is he coming out today?"

"Nah. He's still sick. Puking and everything. So what did you do last night?" Marcel asked.

"Huh? Oh. I saw my uncle's Charger. It's hot as hell."

That night, Akil couldn't sleep. He kept thinking about Tre. How he liked Patrice now. What could Akil do?

6

It was Monday morning. Akil stepped out of his building. Patrice was waiting on the steps. "Want to walk together?"

"Sure," Akil said. Patrice looked great. She didn't try too hard. That was her secret.

They stood outside the school. Akil wished Patrice luck. "I got this," she joked. "Hey, want to eat with me?"

"Sure," Akil said.

"All right. I'll see you at lunch," Patrice winked. Then she headed inside.

Akil couldn't focus. He didn't hear a thing in class. Where should they sit at lunch? Not at his usual table. Tre would be there. Akil wanted to eat with Patrice. Just not at school.

The lunch bell rang. Akil found Patrice. She was talking with Marcel. The three of them loaded up their trays. Marcel led the way. He walked right to their table.

"Here we go," Akil thought.

Marcel, Patrice, and Akil sat down. Deena and Tre joined them.

"Who is this?" Deena said. She glared at Patrice.

"This is Patrice," Marcel said. "Patrice, Deena."

"I remember you, " Patrice said. She tried to be nice. "Same middle school, right?"

"I don't remember you," Deena snapped.

The table was silent. Tre didn't notice. "You missed out, Akil. Marcel and me, we got tore up. Saturday night, man. It was nuts."

"I heard," Akil said.

"Did ya, Akil?" Deena said. "Maybe you heard this too." She stared at Patrice. "Tre is my man. No female better even look his way. I mean even look at him."

Patrice stared right back. She never was one to back down. "I've lost my appetite," she said. She stood up with her tray.

"Me too," Akil said. He followed Patrice.

"What is her problem?" Patrice asked Akil.

"I don't know, Patrice. She's a crazy slut. That's all."

The bell rang. Patrice went to her class. Akil went to his. Again, his mind drifted. "I have to warn her," he thought.

Akil knew Patrice. He knew she would stand up. But that wasn't smart. Deena was crazy. Akil had to tell her. He would tell her after class.

The bell rang. Akil went to find Patrice. It wasn't hard. There was a circle around her and Deena.

Deena screamed and pointed. Then she slammed Patrice against a locker.

Patrice hit the locker hard. She grabbed Deena's hair. Pretty soon they were on the ground. Akil didn't think. He jumped into the mix.

Akil grabbed Deena's arms. He held them behind her back. "Let me go," Deena screamed. "I'm going to kill that girl!"

7

After school, Akil met Marcel and
Tre. They wanted all the details.
"Then what happened?" Marcel
asked.

"Then some teachers came. They
broke it up. That's it." Akil said.

Tre put his fist up to his mouth.
He was laughing. "Deena is crazy
right? I mean crazy! How did she
know? That I want the new girl?"

"Are you serious?" Marcel yelled. "Saturday night? When you couldn't shut up? Kept talking about Patrice? Come on, man."

Tre kept laughing. "Akil, you better look out. Deena is mad at you. You got on her bad side."

"Like I care," Akil said.

"You got something to say about Deena?"

"Whatever."

"That's what I thought."

Akil walked home. He hoped Uncle Robert was there. But his car was gone. Akil climbed the stairs. He stopped at Patrice's floor. Then he kept on going.

His mom was on the couch. "Hey, Ma" he said quietly.

"Hi, baby. How was your day?"

"Okay," he said. Then he walked to his room.

"You need anything, baby? Everything okay?"

Akil stopped. She couldn't see him. He stood in the hallway. Should he tell her about the fight? No. She had enough worries.

"Everything's okay, Ma. I'm going to rest."

But things were not okay. Akil was in bad shape. He tried to write about it. But he couldn't. He didn't go to school on Tuesday. Or Wednesday. He didn't even answer the phone. It was Wednesday night. Akil's mom came in his room. "You got a call, baby. It's Marcel again."

Akil answered. Marcel was his friend. He couldn't hide forever.

They met on the street. Akil didn't say much. Marcel understood. They walked down the block. Soon they were by the court. "Hey, is that your uncle?" Marcel asked.

"Yeah, and Patrice too."

Patrice was shooting from the baseline. It really was her spot. The boys watched her. She made nine shots in a row.

"Damn, Patrice!" Marcel shouted. "You are on fire!"

"Ain't she?" said Uncle Robert. He passed the ball to Marcel. Marcel made a funny move. He tried to fake out Uncle Robert. He shot and missed.

Uncle Robert caught the ball. "Girl can drain 'em all day!"

He passed the ball to Patrice. She didn't shoot. She held onto it. "It's easy out here, Uncle Robert. There's no pressure. Some people crack under pressure."

Patrice passed the ball to Akil. She threw it as hard as she could. "Isn't that right, Akil?"

8

It was Thursday. Akil was quiet at school. He snuck through the halls. He didn't want to see Patrice. It worked until lunch. He saw her eating alone. She sat near the wall.

"Been like that all week," Marcel said.

"What do you mean?"

"Deena can hurt a girl. That's what I mean," Marcel said. A pain went to Akil's heart. He hated seeing Patrice like that. But what could he do? Plus, she was grown. If she needed him, she would ask.

"Deena's got a plan," Marcel said. "Something for Friday. She's gonna get at Patrice again. Damn, here she comes."

Tre and Deena sat down. "Akil, your uncle has a Charger?" Tre asked.

"That's right."

"You gotta get those keys. We need that car, son."

"Get off it," Akil replied.

"When you gonna man up, Akil? That's your problem. You never man up. Never get what you want."

Akil walked home after school.

Uncle Robert was there. "I got something for you," he said. He handed Akil a journal. It had a black leather cover. "It's a late birthday present."

Akil ran his hand on the cover. "Thanks, Uncle Robert," he said.

"It might help you. You know, work things out."

Akil got angry. "What things?"

"Patrice told me about the fight. I know you missed some school. Your mom said you write. I just ..."

"Mom and me are fine, Robert. We were before you got here. We'll be fine when you leave too. Play daddy somewhere else."

Akil threw the journal into a chair. He went to his room. Patrice was talking behind his back. He couldn't believe it. He stayed in his room all night.

Akil met Tre and Marcel the next morning. The boys stood near their lockers. It was Friday. Time to make plans for the night.

"Get this, Akil. Deena's having a girl party tonight. No guys. So we're having a boys' night," Marcel said.

"Perfect night for a ride," Akil said. "I'm taking the Charger out. Tonight's the night."

"My man!" Tre squealed.

Akil felt good. He felt in control. He didn't see Patrice until lunch. She was sitting with some girls. They were from the basketball team.

"So she took his advice," Akil thought.

Akil went home after school. His mom was washing dishes. "Where's Uncle Robert?" Akil asked.

"He's working. He'll be home later tonight. Why?"

Akil felt a rush. His plan was going to work.

"No reason," Akil said. He went to his room. He soon fell asleep. But he didn't mean to.

9

Akil woke up with a start. How long had he been sleeping? He looked at his watch. It was 10:45 PM. He walked to the bathroom. He looked in the mirror. "Damn," he said. His shirt looked awful. He couldn't go out like that!

He could put it in the dryer. That might help. Akil grabbed a quarter.

He tiptoed to the living room. Uncle Robert was already asleep.

Akil made his way down the stairs. On the way, he saw Patrice's mom. She was carrying a basket of clothes.

"Hey, Ma" he said. "Need help?"

"Oh, I'm fine, Akil," she said. "I feel great to tell you the truth."

"Yeah?" Akil asked. "How's that?"

"You know that nasty Deena? The one who picks on Patrice?"

Akil's heart sank.

"Well, she's changed. Wants to be friends now! She even invited my baby to her place. A girls' night after Patrice's game. Can you even believe it? Girl wanted to tear her apart days ago. Now they're pals!"

"Patrice ain't going, is she?" Akil asked. But he knew the answer.

Akil forgot about the dryer. He went back up to his room. He couldn't think. His mind was racing. He called Marcel.

"Hey. My crib. Ten minutes. Call Tre."

It was time. Akil saw Uncle Robert's keys on the table. He held his breath and grabbed them. He held the keys tightly. He didn't let them make noise. Akil snuck out of the apartment. He moved quietly down the stairs.

Akil made it to the street. Then he took a big breath. He tried to act normal. He walked up to the Charger. He got inside.

Akil put his forehead on the wheel. In his mind, he could see Patrice. She was smiling. Like when she hugged him on the street. Then he imagined her alone at lunch.

Akil lifted his head. He looked in the mirror. He saw Marcel and Tre. They were a block away. He started the engine.

10

Akil put the car in drive. What a rush! He pulled away from the curb. He was taking control!

He didn't pick up Tre and Marcel. He was driving to the school.

The school lot was empty. Akil parked and waited. He watched for Patrice's bus. Finally he saw it.

But he also saw red and blue lights. There was a cop behind him!

"Why are you here?" the cop asked.

"I'm ... waiting for my girl," Akil said. It felt good to call Patrice his girl. Even if he was talking to a cop.

"Does she know you're picking her up?" the cop asked.

Akil thought about telling the truth. About what a fool he'd been that week. Just then Patrice ran up.

"You know him?" asked the cop.

She didn't miss a beat. "Yep, he's my neighbor. We won, 94 to 72!"

"That's great, young lady! You kids drive safe now."

Patrice got in the car. She was not happy. "You best get this car back, Akil. You don't have a license."

They drove home without talking.

Akil parked. "Patrice, I'm sorry about this week. I wasn't there for you."

"Save it, Akil. I need to get to Deena's."

"Deena doesn't want to be your friend. The party's a trick, Patrice. I'm sorry you believed her."

Patrice looked out at the street. Then she began to cry. "I hate it here," she said. "I want to go back to my grandma's. I hate my drunk mom. I hate that witch Deena. I can't trust anyone here."

"You can trust me, Patrice."

Patrice turned and stared at him. "You left me this week, Akil."

"I know. I got scared. I ..." He touched her shoulder.

47

"I'm ready now, Patrice," Akil said. "I'm not scared."

Patrice believed him. She leaned across the seat. She kissed him softly. Then she jumped out of the car. Patrice ran into their building.

Akil felt light and warm. He looked up the street. He thought about Tre and Marcel. Akil knew Marcel would understand. He knew Tre wouldn't. But Akil was ready to deal with Tre. It wouldn't be easy. But he was ready.

Inside, Uncle Robert was still asleep. Akil smiled. He sat on the side of the couch. "Uncle Robert. I want to tell you something. You might be mad. But you might be proud too."